Tales from the Bloated Goat

DESIGNED AND PRODUCED BY CARL HERTZOG

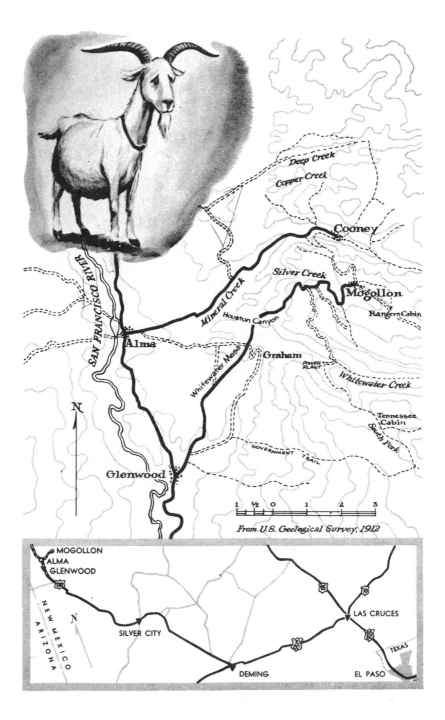

Deep Creek
Copper Creek
Cooney
Silver Creek
Mineral Creek
Mogollon
SAN FRANCISCO RIVER
Houston Canyon
Rangers Cabin
Alma
Whitewater Mesa
Graham
POWER PLANT
Whitewater Creek
N
Tennessee Cabin
South Fork
GOVERNMENT TRAIL
Glenwood

1 ½ 0 1 2 3

From U.S. Geological Survey, 1912

MOGOLLON
ALMA
GLENWOOD
NEW MEXICO
ARIZONA
N
SILVER CITY
LAS CRUCES
TEXAS
DEMING
EL PASO

PUBLISHER'S NOTE

The author, Herman A. Hoover, died suddenly
on January 12, 1958, while this book was "on
the press." He was at the home of his brother
in Goshen, Indiana.

The book was planned for release at Christmas
time, 1957, but was delayed for procurement
of additional photographs. Mr. Hoover stopped
in El Paso on his way to see his folks in Indiana
for Christmas. Only half the pages had been
printed so we took proofs of pages and pictures
and made up one special copy for him to take
on his trip. He did not get to see the finished
book but he did see what it was going to look
like, and he had enjoyed being an author.

— CARL HERTZOG

TALES FROM THE BLOATED GOAT

Early Days In Mogollón

by

H. A. Hoover

Notes and Introduction by

Francis L. Fugate

1958 : Texas Western Press : El Paso

Reprinted By:
High-Lonesome Books
San Lorenzo, New Mexico
88057

H. A. HOOVER
June 15, 1906
This photograph of the author was taken at Silver City when he was returning to the Mogollons after a trip to Indiana.

The author on porch of mine office near Mogollon preparing to embark upon a fishing trip, July, 1936.

INTRODUCTION

THERE WAS A TIME in Mogollon, New Mexico, when the old-timers gathered regularly in the convivial atmosphere of the Bloated Goat to swap yarns about those turbulent days before New Mexico became a state and before Mogollon became a ghost town: Stories of good men and badmen, stories of gold and of animals. Not many of these stories ever escaped from that tight little circle of old settlers. The approach of a stranger, particularly a curious stranger, was a signal for the discussion to veer off aimlessly toward the idiosyncrasies of the weather

That saloon with its waggish eponym was short-lived. Today the Bloated Goat no longer exists as a commercial establishment dedicated to the promotion of good-fellowship; it is gone as a material place of gathering, but its asomatous spirit lives on. If you are lucky you can find that spirit tucked away in the rugged patch of mountains known as the Mogollons; you can find it most any place and most any time when there's a gathering of that ever-decreasing circle of old-timers. If you find it and if you are not too much of a dude and if you know how to listen to the willy-nilly way of now-that-reminds-me talk, the chances are you'll glean a smattering of that old-time lore.

H. A. Hoover is a member in good standing of that exclusive fraternity at the Bloated Goat. He came to the Mogollons in 1904. He paid his initiation fee in the hardships of primitive life in the rugged little mining towns that dotted the canyons of the mountain range. Now, at the age of seventy-seven, you might say he calls the meetings to order.

Mr. Hoover is in a unique position to recount the stories which have circulated about that circle at the Bloated Goat. For more than fifty years he has kept a diary. There are few who can produce a written daily record of their lives for the last half century. His diary was not started or maintained with the idea of publication; it is simply a record of passing events.

"Late in 1902 the thought occurred to me to keep a diary," Mr. Hoover explains, "just why, I do not recall. I bought a small one, cloth bound, three days to the page, and on January 1, 1903, began writing in it. In December of that year I bought one for 1904, more elaborate, bound in flexible leather, with two days to the page. In later years, when available, I always got them with one day to the page. By the time my second diary was filled I had been in New Mexico about eight months and the matter of writing each day's events had become a habit."

Anyone who has ever hunkered down by a campfire or partaken of the camaraderie of tavern conversation will recognize *Tales from the Bloated Goat* for exactly what it is. It makes no pretense of being a complete treatise on any subject it touches, but it fills in many valuable details of a picture that has almost faded. It is a series of relaxed, intimate glimpses of people, places and events of the past—a past which was almost inaccessible by road and which was absolutely forbidden to a prying stranger with a ready notebook and pencil.

Refreshed by entries from his diaries and from the memories of other old-timers at the Bloated Goat, Mr. Hoover has written of those early days: Of desperadoes, of Indians, and of just plain life during those roaring days when the staples of life came into the mountains behind 24-horse teams and coffin handles were a standard item at the general store. Sometimes the accounts do not concur with what historians have said on the same subjects. The historians did not have access to the contemporary notations in Mr. Hoover's diaries, and it can be assumed that talk turned to the weather when they dropped in at the Bloated Goat. —FRANCIS L. FUGATE

FOREWORD

THE RANGE OF MOUNTAINS known as "The Mogollons" (locally pronounced "Muggy-yones") lies in southwestern New Mexico, about ten miles from the Arizona state line, extending roughly fifty miles north and south by twenty-five miles east and west; most of the area is contained in the Gila National Forest.* For majestic grandeur this range will compare favorably with any other range in the Rockies.

Any painting is made up of innumerable small strokes of the artist's brush, the aggregate composing a picture of the subject at hand. Likewise, while each of the incidents related herein is of itself more or less trivial, combined they form a word picture of early-day life in the Mogollons.

I was raised in a religious element very literal in its interpretation of the Scriptures and had always supposed that some day I would become a member of that church. But after being out here in the mountains for a few weeks, where I saw and studied the magnificent work of the Creator, I one day realized that something had happened to me: My mind felt like it was unshackled and I had a buoyancy of spirit I never knew before. To this day, my only "church" is out under the Blue Dome where one can communicate alone with his Maker.

Looking back now, I think of Arthur Chapman's classic poem "Out Where the West Begins," a line of which runs "Where . . . a man makes friends without half trying." More than fifty years ago, during my short stop in Silver City while en route out here, my first contact with local people was a revelation in the immediate friendly spirit with which a newcomer was accepted.

For some of the pictures and other material in this book I am indebted to Fritz A. Aude, Mrs. E. M. Coates, E. A. Cunningham, E. D. McIntosh, W. Irvin Moore, and Len Shellhorn—all old-time residents hereabouts; Charles B. Barker, the late J. Marvin Hunter, Sr., T. J. "Shorty" Lyon, Philip J. Rasch and George Fitzpatrick of *New Mexico* magazine.

Especial gratitude is due Louis Jones of Glenwood, without whose help the details of some of these unusual events might be lost forever.

Mogollon, New Mexico
May 15, 1957

—H. A. HOOVER

* The mountain range was named by the early Spanish explorers to honor Señor Don Juan Ignacio Flores Mogollón, who was "governor and captain-general of this kingdom and provinces of New Mexico and warden of its forces and presidios for his majesty" during the early part of the eighteenth century.

CONTENTS

I. Early-Day Life in a Western Mining Camp . . . 11

"Homeseekers' Excursion" — 13; I Got a Job — 16; A Deferred Pay Day — 18; Short Rations — 19; I take a Vacation — 23; Early Batching Days — 25; New Mining Operation Starts — 26; We Get the Telephone—30; My First Ride in an Auto—31; Roadside Dental and Optical Service — 33; Statehood — 33; The "Flu" Epidemic — 34; Glenwood — 34.

II. Days of Death and Violence 37

Some Tales of Indian Days — 39; A Kangaroo Court in Cooney — 40; The Freeman-Clark Murder — 41; Some Other Killings—Illegal and Otherwise — 43; The Hollimon-Hannigan Affair — 48; William McGinnis: Train Robber—49; The Killing of Ralph Jenks—53; Another Stage Holdup — 56; Ben Lilly: Lion Hunter — 57.

III. Today in the Mogollons 59

PHOTOGRAPHS

H. A. Hoover in 1906 and in 1936 6

Mogollon traffic 45 years ago 11

Montgomery Ward & Co. catalogue of 1904 14

Godfrey and his primitive restaurant 21

The whiskey-barrel waterworks 21

Views of Alma, Cooney, and Mogollon 22

Freighting over mountain curves 27-28

Cooney, New Mexico, in 1904 37

View from the Little Fanney Mine 38

Election Day in Cooney 44

William H. Antrim 51

Ben Lilly, the lion hunter 54

The author on Whitewater Mesa, 1956 59

Mogollon mountain scenery 62

I

Everyday Life in a Western Mining Camp

Mogollon traffic 45 years ago

NOTE: *The large italics at the beginning of various articles and interspersed throughout the text indicate exact quotations from Mr. Hoover's diary.*

"HOMESEEKERS' EXCURSION"

MARCH 14, 1904: *Have definitely made up my mind to start for New Mexico about April 1st. Am making preparations.*

IN THE SUMMER OF 1902 I had gone to work on a hydroelectric power installation on the St. Joe River, about six miles east of South Bend, Indiana, and but a few miles from my farm home. It was there I met M. L. Bugbee who had come from the East on the staff of the contractors for the project. We became close friends. In the fall of 1903 Bugbee went West for his health and finally landed in Cooney, New Mexico, about three miles across the mountains from Mogollon.

The construction job in Indiana was completed in March, 1904. My friend Bugbee had become manager for the only store in Cooney, owned by the Mogollon Gold & Copper Company, then operating the original mineral discovery in this district. We corresponded regularly, and that spring Bugbee invited me to come out here. Being young and foot-loose and of an adventurous nature, I decided to do so.

I wrote the Santa Fe Railway about rates, and they advised me of a "Homeseekers' Excursion" to leave Chicago April 5, 1904, the fare to Deming, New Mexico, being $23.75.* Between trains in Chicago I went to Montgomery Ward & Company's store—their only one at the time—and bought a Smith & Wesson .32 caliber hammerless pistol and a box of ca'tridges, loaded it and carried it in a hip pocket, believing that in the "wild and woolly West" it might be needed. Arriving here, I soon realized it would have been more useful back in Indiana; it certainly would not have stood up long against the big .45's then in vogue here.

I cannot imagine any future trip having more fascination than my initial journey to the West: My first ride in a Pullman; the marvelous meals in those Harvey Houses en route; my first sight of a mountain, snow-clad Pike's Peak as it slowly arose over the horizon; the train laboring up Raton Pass with two locomotives pulling and one pushing; stopping at the summit, the porter closing our windows and turning on the lights while two engines were detached; going through that long, dark tunnel, then the rapid glide down other side of mountain; my astonishment at the sight of a woman astride a horse as the train rolled into Las Vegas—where I came from, when women rode a horse at all it was on a sidesaddle.

At Albuquerque we changed to the A. T. & S. F. branch running to

---

* The current one-way Pullman fare from Chicago to Deming, tax included, is $83.23.

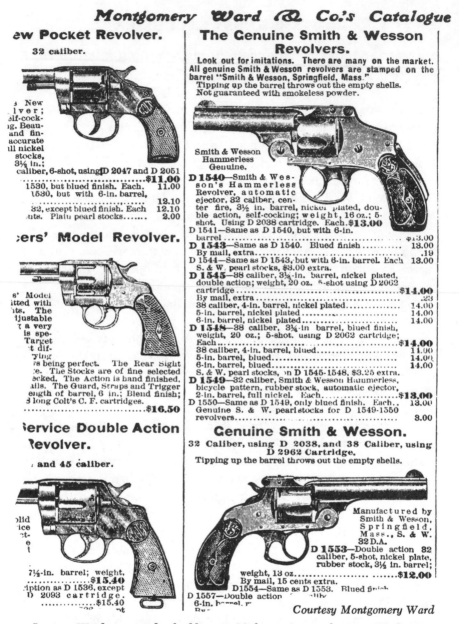

ew Pocket Revolver.

32 caliber.

3 New
lver;
elf-cock-
ig. Beau-
and fin-
accurate
ll nickel
stocks,
3½ in.;
caliber, 6-shot, using D 2047 and D 2051
...........................**$11.00**
1530, but blued finish. Each   11.00
1530, but with 6-in. barrel,
....   12.10
32, except blued finish. Each   12.10
.uts. Plain pearl stocks....... 2.00

ers' Model Revolver.

s' Model
itted with
its. The
ljustable
₹ a very
is spe-
Target
t dif-
rying
79 being perfect. The Rear Sight
:e. The Stocks are of fine selected
acked. The Action is hand finished,
ails. The Guard, Straps and Trigger
ength of barrel, 6 in.; Blend finish;
3 long Colt's C. F. cartridges.
.............................**$16.50**

Service Double Action
Revolver.

. and 45 caliber.

olid
ice
:t-
t
7½-in. barrel; weight,
...............**$15.40**
iption as D 1536, except
D 2093 cartridge.
..............$15.40

The Genuine Smith & Wesson Revolvers.

Look out for imitations. There are many on the market.
All genuine Smith & Wesson revolvers are stamped on the
barrel "Smith & Wesson, Springfield, Mass."
Tipping up the barrel throws out the empty shells.
Not guaranteed with smokeless powder.

Smith & Wesson
Hammerless
Genuine.

D 1540—Smith & Wes-
son's Hammerless
Revolver, automatic
ejector, 32 caliber, cen-
ter fire, 3½ in. barrel, nickel plated, double action, self-cocking; weight, 16 oz.; 5-
shot. Using D 2038 cartridge. Each.**$13.00**
D 1541—Same as D 1540, but with 6-in.
barrel.............................. $13.00
D 1543—Same as D 1540. Blued finish........... 13.00
By mail, extra.................................. .19
D 1544—Same as D 1543, but with 6-in. barrel. Each 13.00
S. & W. pearl stocks, $3.00 extra.
D 1545—38 caliber, 3½-in. barrel, nickel plated,
double action; weight, 20 oz. 5-shot using D 2062
cartridge.......................................**$14.00**
By mail, extra............................... .23
38 caliber, 4-in. barrel, nickel plated.............. 14.00
5-in. barrel, nickel plated 14.00
6-in. barrel, nickel plated 14.00
D 1548—38 caliber, 3¼-in barrel, blued finish,
weight, 20 oz.; 5-shot. using D 2062 cartridge,
Each...**$14.00**
38 caliber, 4-in. barrel, blued........................ 14.00
5-in. barrel, blued................................ 14.00
6-in. barrel, blued................................ 14.00
S. & W. pearl stocks, on D 1545-1548, $3.25 extra.
D 1549—32 caliber, Smith & Wesson Hammerless,
bicycle pattern, rubber stock, automatic ejector,
2-in. barrel, full nickel. Each....................**$13.00**
D 1550—Same as D 1549, only blued finish. Each.. 13.00
Genuine S. & W. pearl stocks for D 1549-1550
revolvers....................................... 3.00

Genuine Smith & Wesson.

32 Caliber, using D 2038, and 38 Caliber, using
D 2962 Cartridge.
Tipping up the barrel throws out the empty shells.

Manufactured by
Smith & Wesson,
Springfield,
Mass., S. & W.
32 D.A.

D 1553—Double action 32
caliber, 5-shot, nickel plate,
rubber stock, 3½ in. barrel;
weight, 13 oz.................. ......**$12.00**
By mail, 15 cents extra.
D 1554—Same as D 1553. Blued finish
D 1557—Double action
6-in. barrel.

Courtesy Montgomery Ward

In 1904 Wards occupied a building on Michigan Avenue between Washington
and Madison Streets. The building covered the entire block and was known as the
"Ward Tower Building," because its tower was at that time the tallest structure of
its kind west of the Alleghenies.

Citizens of Chicago could not buy from Wards "over the counter." But customers
from out of town were served. They selected what they wanted from the catalog
and after a short wait the merchandise was delivered to them if it was such that they
could and wished to take it with them. A clerk wrote the customer's order and sent
it through just the same as an order received by mail.

El Paso, and at Rincon we transferred to another train on the line from there to Silver City, where I arrived about 1 P.M. on Friday, April 8th. On a previous suggestion from Bugbee I went to the Palace Hotel (now the Monterey) and found a letter from him with introductions to three businessmen there.

I stayed over until the Monday morning stage. In those days gambling of all sorts was wide open in the Territory. I had never before seen so much money at one time—great stacks of gold and silver, piles of paper currency. Every barroom was equipped for a wide variety of gambling. They were open from January 1st to December 31st. In 1907 when the Territorial legislature outlawed gambling, to take effect January 1, 1908, many of the bars had been open continuously for so many years that no one knew where to find the keys to their doors; locks had to be replaced.

Among my letters of introduction was one to C. W. Marriott, express agent, operator of the stage line to Mogollon and Cooney, and mail contractor to those points. The stage also carried passengers. On Saturday I engaged a seat on the stage to Cooney for Monday morning. The fare was $10, nearly half as much as I had paid from Chicago to Deming!

One might visualize this "stage" as a clumsy, lumbering affair, with the driver on a high, outside seat, driving two or three span of horses, like the many pictures of pioneer days in the West. This one, however, was just a large, two-seated buggy with a long body extension in back to accommodate mail and express. It had a square top, mounted on four corner posts and covered with canvas, the sides and rear end rolled up except when the weather was stormy. It had only two horses and they trotted almost continuously except on the upgrades.

We left Silver City at 7:15 on the morning of April 11th and changed horses about every twenty miles, the first change being at Mangas, then at Warm Springs, next at "Pa" Meader's on Big Dry Creek, and at Whitewater (now known as Glenwood). A fresh team was always in harness, hitched to a rack, as we drove up to a station, and it was but a few minutes until we were again on the way. A time or two they greased the axles of the stage at a station.

The driver that day was Jake House, a picturesque character who delighted in reciting earlier history of the area to newcomers, pointing out, among other things, the bones of several horses of soldiers who had been waylaid by Indians on Little Dry Creek some twenty years previously. It was then known as "Soldier Hill." This driver went only as far as Whitewater. Then a fresh team, stage and driver went on to Mogollon, and still another conveyance went to Alma, up Mineral Creek and through Cooney Canyon to the mining camp of Cooney,* where we arrived about 8:15 P.M. after thirteen hours on the road. Speedometers now clock the distance from Silver City out here at around seventy-eight miles, but in those days it was called "ninety miles"—and it seemed all of that after the day-long, rough, dusty trip.

The entries in my diary reveal that my first reaction to Cooney was not favorable:

APRIL 12, 1904 (The day after my arrival): *This is nothing but a mining camp in a great deep canyon about 800 feet high. Steep rocky walls. Don't know how I'll like it. Feel disappointed now.*

APRIL 15: *Quite windy. Wind only blows 2 ways here—up and down canyon. Blows up mostly in daytime. I don't like this place any better than I did. I feel homesick or something.*

APRIL 19: *Have not got the blues so bad as I had. Think I will like the country all right.*

Apparently I learned to "like" it, for over fifty years later I find myself only about two miles from what was then Cooney, deeply rooted in the country!

I GOT A JOB

MAY 5, 1904: *Began working for Cooney Mercantile Co. in store today @ 2 bucks per day. Like it all right for start.*

MY FIRST EMPLOYMENT in the country was clerking in the Cooney store. It was a "general merchandise" establishment, carrying groceries, dry goods, men's suits made-to-order, boots and shoes, hats, light hardware, cigars and tobacco, bottled drugs and patent medicines, beer, wine and whiskey, with even a small homemade bar in the rear where the clerk was now and then required to serve drinks.

The beer came in large bottles, enough for several glasses, and when a customer was served any left in the bottle was corked to await the next man. Without refrigeration of any kind, the stuff was naturally at the temperature of the atmosphere. One day two cowboys came in and asked for beer. I set out the glasses, opened a bottle, and in my country-boy ignorance started pouring with the mouth of the bottle a couple of inches from the top of the tumbler. It being warm weather, the glass was all foam from bottom to top.

"You shore never poured much beer!" one of the lads said to me.

---

* Named for James C. Cooney, an Army sergeant stationed in the vicinity who made the first gold strike in the canyon during the 1870's. See "Some Tales of Indian Days," page 39.

Coffin handles were a standard item among the hardware. When a death occurred in the community some carpenter would fashion a crude coffin out of rough lumber. The store carried a special black cloth to cover the outside and a white material with which to line the inside. Then those coffin handles were screwed on. I will never forget with what reluctance I even touched them in passing those handles over the counter!

A stranger standing around the store a few hours on some days might get the impression we were not doing much business. Then perhaps a rancher or stockman would come in and buy $50 or $75 worth—and in those days such sums bought a lot. One day a sheepman came in with a pack outfit. After I had filled his order of miscellaneous items, he inquired what we had in work shoes. I showed him. Then he produced an extra-large gunny sack and came around between the front and rear counters. I straddled the aisle with one foot on each counter and emptied the long shelf of shoes while he held the mouth of the sack open for me to dump them in. Sizes were not considered.

MAY 16, 1904: *Trouble in camp. Bugbee is going to resign his position.*

MAY 17: *Bugbee and Masten had long talk, final. Bug. is giving up management of store . . . I will have to "vamoose" soon, also Rosenfeld.*

In the summer of 1904 the Mogollon Gold & Copper Company changed managers of its mining operations and since the manager directed the company store, the new man relieved Bugbee of his job. Later his successor hired other clerks; however, I was kept on the job longer than I had anticipated.

AUGUST 13, 1904: *Last day for me in store. Hoorah.*

In August I went to work for Cooney & Weatherby (Thomas F. Cooney and William J. Weatherby, both now deceased), mining engineers whose efforts during the next few years meant a great deal to the prosperity of the Cooney Mining District, as this locality came to be known officially in the State mining records. My work for them at that time was little more than nominal, hence I continued in the store until August 13th.

A. G. "Duffy" Morrow was the postmaster at Cooney. He took a three-month leave of absence, and on September 5 I was sworn in as acting postmaster to serve until Morrow's return in December, this job to run "concurrently" with my other. According to my diary notation the work must not have been onerous.

SEPTEMBER 16, 1904: *This P.O. business is damned tiresome —nothing to do but read.*

Under normal weather conditions the mail arrived by stage about 8:30 P.M. and was at once distributed. Most of the patrons got theirs immediately. The arrival of the mail was usually the main event of the day with about all of the adult population assembling near the post office before the stage came in. While waiting for the mail they discussed with one another whatever was of greatest interest at the time. The outgoing mail was then put up and it left about 1:30 or 2 o'clock in the morning. The stage driver had a key to the post office so that the postmaster did not have to be there in the wee hours; hence, during the day it was mostly a job of killing time.

On paydays and for a day or two after there would be a spurt of money order business. While in that office I saw a $100 bill for the first time. Until I became acting postmaster so far as I was concerned a piece of currency meant only what it said on its face: A $5 or $10 bill was only that. But while being coached for the office I found out there was more to it. There were National Bank currency, Federal currency, Gold Certificates, Silver Certificates, and maybe others. Each bill had its own individual number, all of which had to be recorded when it was transmitted to the regional office at Albuquerque.

DECEMBER 12, 1904: *Morrow came in at 11 and we counted stamps, etc., till 1 and worked till 5 settling up. (Got all balled up.) Met at 7:30 and finished up at 9. I owe him $20.38 (overdrew).*

A DEFERRED PAY DAY

JANUARY 1, 1905: *Men held mass meeting in saloon this P.M. and called upon M G & C Co. to pay up at once. Armed men out all night watching that they don't leave camp.*

UP UNTIL THIRTY YEARS AGO, more or less, the mining companies in this district paid off only once a month, on the twentieth for the calendar month preceding. Thus, if a man went to work on May 1st, he had no pay check until June 20th. But it was always arranged that he had credit at the boarding- and roominghouse, as well as at a store, and if a man looked all right the saloons would chalk up his drinks. Hence, ready pocket money was not so essential to one's daily comfort.

On December 20, 1904, the Mogollon Gold & Copper Company in Cooney was unable to meet its payroll. Naturally, the men were uneasy. They wandered around, not knowing what to do about the situation. T. J. Curran, the president of the company, and a Mr. Masten, the treasurer, were in Cooney from New York. As revealed by my diary, the men held a mass meeting on New Year's day; after that "armed men" were "watching" to see that the company officials did not get away on the stage which left after midnight.

JANUARY 3, 1905: *"Posse" of men following Masten and Curran to see that they did not get off.*

That was during the day. There was no indication that these company officials intended to leave camp without paying the men, but they were taking no chances!

In those days the payroll funds for struggling companies were usually mailed from the East to the bank in Silver City. With no telephone service, the company had to await advice of the deposit by mail. News of the deposit in Silver City must have arrived in the mail on the evening of January 3rd.

JANUARY 4: *M G & C Co. giving out checks.*

Thus ended the trouble, and I'll wager not a man in the camp was happier than Mr. Curran and Mr. Masten.

SHORT RATIONS

MARCH 3, 1905: *Bugbee was in a while. He feels blue about scarcity of grub and horse feed.*

THE LATTER PART OF 1904 and the early winter and spring of 1905 were excessively wet: Rain, rain, and more rain. All of the roads in the country in those days were just as Nature had made them. Long stretches were of clay or adobe and became impassable to anything but the lightest vehicles. Freight wagons would sink to the axles. The Whitewater Mesa, just below Mogollon, was so wet I heard a cowhand remark, "It will bog a saddle blanket."

There was no bridge across the Gila River and the stream ran bank-high for long periods. The crossing at Red Barn [Gila] was better than that near Riverside. A steel cable had been strung across the river at the Red Barn by mounting the ends on a high post at either side. A platform, only a few feet square, hung from a small trolley on the cable.

The stage from Silver City would stop on its side of the river and put the mail and small packages on the platform. Then by a rope attached to it a man on the other side would pull it across. Thus the Silver City and Mogollon stages would exchange mail and back-track. Even with the convenience of that cable, frequently there was a week at a time when we got no mail at Mogollon or Cooney due to the super-soft roads. With no telephone connections we were pretty thoroughly isolated from the outside world. After weeks of no freight at all there was some apprehension as to the food supply.

But there was never any danger of famine as the stores had a modest supply of some essentials, such as beans, salt pork and coffee. There was always plenty of beef-on-the-hoof around the mountains and, in a pinch, wild game. If there were any game laws then no one observed them; first one and then another would bring me a piece of venison in all seasons of the year except mid-summer when it would not keep so well.

However, during that wet period we did run out of one big item— flour. All the stores in Mogollon, Alma and Cooney were cleaned out of it. At that time there was a German, Godfrey Remele, who ran a very primitive restaurant in Cooney. Only a few knew him by any other name than Godfrey. He sold bread regularly to a few of us, but he too ran out of flour. The main thing I remember about it now is how quickly I became accustomed to not having bread; I did not even miss it when there was plenty of other substantial food.

APRIL 4, 1905: *Got bread from Godfrey, first in a month.*

An incident told to me in later years emphasizes the remark that Godfrey's restaurant was "very primitive." My wife's oldest sister, Mrs. Harry M. Ward [now deceased], and her family were living in Cooney. As Godfrey baked every two or three days and had an ample supply of leavening on hand, Mrs. Ward now and then bought yeast from him. One morning she went to the restaurant to get some in a quart jar. He kept it in a wooden candy bucket. Upon removing the lid from the bucket he found a dead mouse in it. The least he could have done was pull it out and throw it away. Instead he picked it out by the tail with one hand; with the thumb and forefinger of the other he stripped the yeast that was sticking to it back into the bucket! Needless to say, Mrs. Ward bought no yeast from him that day nor ever again.

In my purchase of bread from Godfrey it is quite possible that I got a loaf made from that mousy batch of yeast. If so it was not lethal; fifty years later I find myself still in fair condition. "What you don't know won't hurt you" is more truth than poetry.

Godfrey in the doorway of his "very primitive" restaurant.

The Author's Whiskey-Barrel Waterworks.

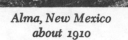

Alma, New Mexico
about 1910

Mogollon
"Main Street"
about 1910

"Business District"
Cooney, New Mexico
1904

I TAKE A VACATION

APRIL 26, 1906: *Duff will take my place while I'm gone.*

BY THE EARLY PART OF 1906 the mine promotion efforts of Cooney & Weatherby had progressed to the point where they started sinking the main shaft of the Little Fanney Mine, and on January 6th I moved from Cooney to that operation, which was near Mogollon. Six burros packed my entire outfit.

There were no wells on the mountain top and the nearest water was at a spring on the side of the canyon road about a half a mile from my cabin. I engaged a boy to pack water to me on a burro; he carried two ten-gallon kegs for 50¢ a trip, or 2½¢ a gallon. In those days whiskey was shipped out here in barrels. I bought an empty fifty-gallon barrel down in Mogollon, had it brought up and put on my porch. Then I caved in the head and my water boy filled it. Of course, for a while it had a slight whiskey taste, but that was not too objectionable!

Those were the years of "forty-rod whiskey," when they would sometimes make two barrels out of one, putting in plugs of tobacco and what-not to give it color and flavor. At least that was the story, although I never found personal proof. However, I was recently talking to an old-timer who recalled an incident many years ago when he knocked in the head of an empty barrel and found several plugs of tobacco on the inside. I never knew whether the name meant that the stuff would affect one if he got within forty rods of it, or whether that was as far as he would get after partaking of it. It was during the period of forty-rod whiskey that I heard a veteran saloon man remark with a chuckle, "If it's good they'll drink it and *praise* it. If it's bad they'll drink it and *curse* it!"

My whiskey-barrel water works system continued until the latter part of 1908 when a pipeline was completed from springs some three miles up in the mountains to the mine where I lived. During the rainy season my water supply was augmented by a rain barrel under the eaves. In those days I really learned to conserve water and I have never gotten over the habit of setting the teakettle on the back of the stove when it begins to boil.

That spring it was decided I was entitled to a vacation. I made arrangements for A. G. Morrow, for whom I had substituted in the Cooney post office two years before, to take my place while I was gone. As the departure date approached, I noted in my diary:

MAY 2, 1906: *Began packing up for trip home.*

The regular stage then left Mogollon about 2 A.M., and the only reason I did not get on it was because it was "sold out" for that trip. However, some time before, Ernest Craig, operator of the Last Chance Mine, had established his own private stage line to Silver City to haul his own bullion. So I took the Craig conveyance on the morning of May 3rd. We left about 5:30 and stopped at Craig's mine to load bullion.

It was just a plain two-seated buggy without a top, so we had the luxury of a bright, hot sun all day. George F. Williams was the driver and I sat in the front seat with him; the rear seat was occupied by a Joe Bustamante and his wife. We changed horses regularly at the stations for the mail stage and everything went on schedule until we were in the edge of Silver City, about 8 P.M.

There was a bright moon straight overhead and no shadows in the road; the land looked level. Even the horses were fooled. They were clopping along with loose reins— Suddenly the buggy began to tip sharply toward the left and in a moment we were all dumped out. The buggy ended up on its side with one set of high wheels pointed at the bright moon. We looked around and found the road was but a few feet below to the left. We tipped the buggy back on its wheels, led the team into the road, put the bullion and baggage aboard, and climbed back in. In a few minutes we were down at the express office where we checked in the bullion.

When I had first arrived in Silver City back in April, 1904, I thought I had about reached the end of the world. But after two years in the mountain villages, the place looked like a metropolis! We had arrived too late for me to catch the train out, so I had all day—May 4th—to visit around town and make new acquaintances.

And right here I want to say a special word for Silver City. I noticed it then and have never failed to observe it since on my periodic trips in and out of there for half a century: Nowhere else have I ever seen and felt the friendliness that seems so spontaneous no matter into what establishment you enter. Maybe it is all of us living on the edge of the clearing that engenders an unconscious feeling of kinship.

During that day I had to call at the bank for cash for my trip back to Indiana. Colonel J. W. Carter, the cashier, met me at the window. He was well acquainted with my employers but knew me only through correspondence. He was a kindly, sociable man. He invited me to come in behind the grill and we visited while he worked at a small table. The bank then had two tellers, Harry and Mason Kelly, brothers. One of them proudly showed me the adding machine they had acquired some time previously.

He said that at first they "wouldn't trust it." They would come down to the bank at night and "practice with it" on long columns of figures "that had been proven." By the time I got there it had gained their confidence and they were putting out good money on its mechanical results.

I arrived in Indiana in due course without incident, going via El Paso and the Rock Island Railway. Nearly the whole country back East was green; in comparison with the semi-arid Southwest it seemed like a vast park. But alas, after a few weeks in that Eden I began to feel like I had a blanket over my head. I was longing for the wide open spaces, "Out Where the West Begins," where one can see a hundred miles and the skies are seldom cloudy all day. I returned via the Santa Fe Railway through Albuquerque.

Those who have lived in New Mexico long enough to learn to love the state—have gone out for a while and come back—will understand the rather boyish observation written in my diary on the train that second morning out of Chicago: *We are well into N. Mex. now. It looks good again, I can tell you.*

Some time after my return to Mogollon I was talking to M. E. Coates, the storekeeper, about my trip. I remarked that I had seen several automobiles back East. In his quaint, drawling voice he said: "They've —got—one—of—them—things—in—Silver City." A while before Colonel W. C. Porterfield, its owner, had given him "a ride in it."

EARLY BATCHING DAYS

FEBRUARY 9, 1905: *Went over to see a cook stove at Garcias.*

I HAD BEEN LIVING with my friend Bugbee and his family in a house across the canyon road from the one I proposed to fix up in which to go "batching." At intervals between February 9th and March 1st I gradually put the place in order and assembled the necessary equipment. From then on until my marriage in 1908, I was on my own at housekeeping.

FEBRUARY 28: *Made several trips to store packing up dishes, etc.*

MARCH 1: *Went over to house and built fire and got breakfast in my new home. First meal not good as the spiders* [as frying pans were then called] *had varnish on inside and made pota-toes and meat bitter.*

During May and June, with endless days of cloudless skies, a week's trip in a freight wagon from Silver City out here often did something to the cargo. Bacon and hams moulded en route: Those big 20- or 25-pound round cheeses were dripping and getting strong by the time we got them; more often than not butter was rancid.

Someone told me that boiling would improve butter. I boiled a pound, skimming off a greenish foam, but it was still hard to swallow. There was no refrigeration here then except for an occasional tunnel into the mountainside. This worked well enough for anything that was in fair condition when placed inside of it, but Arctic Circle temperatures could not have brought that butter back!

However, now and then there were some compensations. Think of this: NOVEMBER 4, 1905: *Got 12 lbs, fine steak at 10¢ from Bill Tate.* Bill now lives in Glenwood and may get a chuckle out of this should he read it.

NEW MINING OPERATION STARTS

APRIL 8, 1908: *Talked with Tom in at Williams—things are looking good.*

APRIL 25: *Mr. Spillsbury, Sully and Tom got here at 11:30.*

JUNE 19: *Letter from Tom says new underwriting is closed.*

JUNE 30: *Tom Cooney came up about 9. We are going to start up at once on the Fanney.*

JULY 1: *Letter from W.J.* [William J. Weatherby] *says to go home for trip at once.*

THOSE ENTRIES FAINTLY TRACED the latter stages of the financing and the beginning of the development of the Little Fanney mine. E. Gibbon Spillsbury, John M. Sulley (who developed the Chino mine at Santa Rita), and Thomas F. Cooney were all mining engineers. By July 1st of that year William J. Weatherby had been in the East over a year promoting the deal. After getting Weatherby's warning I got married on July 11th, left at once for Indiana on a wedding trip, and I returned in August when work had started in earnest.

This involved mine development, erection of a 200-ton milling plant, a three-mile pipeline to springs farther up in the mountains, a three-mile road into Whitewater Creek where a steam power plant was constructed in a timbered area and, as an auxiliary, a pipeline was to be extended

Lower end of Mogollon in its heyday

FREIGHTING OVER MOUNTAIN HAIRPIN CURVES

Tons of heavy equipment were required to work the mines; the only roads were so rough and narrow and steep that they would be impossible even to today's most modern equipment. When the freight was so heavy that several teams were required to pull the load, negotiation of the steep mountain roads became tricky business. On hairpin turns the lead team was often going in the opposite direction of the load to which they were attached. An ingenious hitching arrangement provided that all teams would always be helping to pull the load.

A heavy chain long enough to accommodate the number of teams required to pull the load was attached to the axle of the wagon. The team closest to the wagon was hitched to the wagon's tongue in the customary manner in order that they could steer the vehicle. Other teams were hitched at intervals to the long chain by means of doubletrees attached by short lengths of chain. Thus, their pulling force was transmitted to the long chain which was fastened directly to wagon axle.

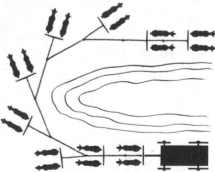

The driver mounted an animal on the lefthand side of the teams. He maintained control by means of a check line which passed through a ring on the hame of each lefthand animal and was fastened to the lead. By manipulation of this check line the driver controlled the lead team, keeping it on the road.

As the front team went around turns, the long chain would rub the legs of one of the animals in the team behind—right or left, depending upon the direction of the curve—and that animal would jump over the chain to get out of its way. Thus the animals were kept on the road and at the same time maintained a pull on the long chain which was attached to the wagon.

up the creek for water power part of the year. Orders for all the machinery and equipment were promptly placed and in course of time began arriving in carload lots in Silver City, our nearest railway point.

At that time W. A. Tenney was the principal freighter in Silver City, but such a mass of freight was beyond his capacity. Our transfer agents, Lowe & Hann, scoured the area for teams and wagons to haul freight to Mogollon. On our end we engaged a man to rustle freighters from among the farmers and ranchers. There were no franchises then and everyone was welcome!

I recall one load of only 1250 pounds which was hauled out by a Mexican boy with two horses. Since he was paid $1.25 per hundred pounds and his team probably did not require much feed, he may have cleared a dollar a day for that trip. A lot of freight was in sizes and weights that could be handled by the smaller outfits, but in other cases single pieces ran into the tons. Only Tenney was prepared to handle this class of freight which required especially heavy wagons with from sixteen to twenty-four horses attached.

About that time I read a comment in one of the Silver City papers to the effect that it took more ingenuity to pilot a train of horses like that over these crooked mountain roads with their hairpin turns than it took to steer a ship across the Atlantic. Anyone witnessing the feat would heartily agree. Even today, a visitor now and then seeing this machinery in place seems a bit skeptical that it could have been hauled in by wagon.

By 1910 mining operations in the Mogollons were under way on a large scale, reaching their peak about 1912-1915. Naturally the town of Mogollon was booming and having growing pains,* attracting camp followers of both sexes, an element that brought many thorns into the community. In the latter part of July, 1910, three of the transient girls boarded the stage after midnight. When the stage reached the top of a mountain about a mile and a half out it was stopped by a man who ordered the women to get off and then robbed them. The stage driver brought back this tale: After being frisked the girls got back on. Two of them cried, bemoaning their penniless condition; the third told them not to worry, that she had the bulk of her money done up in the long hair on top of her head! The robber was not apprehended.

---

* In a survey of the area, published in 1917, Mogollon was noted as "now the most important place in the district." It had a population of 2000. During the year 1915, $150,000 worth of money orders were sold across the post office counter. Merchants of the town received an aggregate of 60,000 tons of goods during that year.—Ralph E. Twitchell, *The Leading Facts of New Mexican History* (Cedar Rapids, 1917), Vol. IV, p. 290, note.

AUGUST 9, 1910: *The Mogollon stage was held up this morning, driver killed and the bullion taken off. I went to Alma at 11 for news—heard the bullion had all been recovered and that an auto load of blood hounds was on way from Gila.*

Early that morning two Mexicans left Mogollon on foot for the Whitewater power plant, some five miles away. About two miles out of town they *found a dead man in the road with 3 bullet holes in his back. His body was cold.* They returned to Mogollon and reported.

Meanwhile George Rowe, at Glenwood, had dispatched the stage from there to Silver City at the usual time of night. In the morning he phoned up to learn what had happened to the stage out of Mogollon. A group of men then took a short cut up the mountain. They found the dead driver; farther down, the team and stage were standing at the side of the road. Evidently seeing signs that the bullion had been packed into the bushes, they scouted around and found every bar of it, seven from one company and five from another, about $10,000 worth. Just what happened no one will ever know. Although there was strong suspicion as to who did it, no real evidence was ever found.

WE GET THE TELEPHONE

MARCH 3, 1909: *McIntosh got telephone connections with Silver City today.*

IN THE LATTER PART OF 1908 work was started on extending the telephone from Gila to Mogollon. Finally, on March 3rd of the next year, connection was made with the McIntosh store in Mogollon. Later other local stores and the mine offices were hooked up.

The service took in Alma, Glenwood and ranchers who lived beyond. It was strictly a party line, and there must have been twelve or fifteen phones on it. Each subscriber paid $10 per month. One ring would call the Silver City exchange; then we would ask for the number wanted. With so many on the line, it was often busy. And when we put in a call not infrequently we would hear a faint click—eavesdroppers listening in!

But despite those slight annoyances, the telephone gave us a sense of being in touch with the world. And we could send a telegram right now! Previously, a message would be written today, go out on tomorrow's mail, and get to the telegraph office day-after-tomorrow morning. All incoming telegrams of course took the same tedious route.

MY FIRST RIDE IN AN AUTO

NOVEMBER 4, 1907: *In P.M. I packed my suit case to go to Silver City tomorrow . . . got a letter from Tom in mail which will delay my trip a day.*

HOW WELL I REMEMBER the disappointment of the delay; that trip was to be my first ride in an automobile. Bugbee was living in Silver City and he had invited me to come in and spend a week with him. Some automobiles were then being tried out on the mail haul between Mogollon and Silver City. I engaged a seat on a car scheduled to leave at 7 A.M. November 6th. The "depot" was at the Coates store in the lower end of the village. There were four of us to go out. We waited and waited until the car finally came about 8:45.

On the autos of those days tops and windshields were "optional"— this one had neither. As a protection to my eyes I was advised to buy a pair of goggles, which I got from Coates. This machine was a little two-seated Reo, the rear seat much higher than the front. The motor was under the front seat and two telephone batteries furnished the ignition. The car was so short that it could turn around in the narrow down town street.

I sat in the middle of the rear seat with Jake House, the stage driver, on my right and another passenger on my left; the fourth passenger was in front with the driver, young Charlie Marriott, who sat on the right side. There was little leg room in the rear, and after we were seated the mail sacks were wedged in, almost in our laps. They always had to be removed before we could get out. The car had two forward speeds and the gear-shift lever was on the outside of the driver's seat. In low on up-grades it had a habit of jumping out of gear, so Jake would reach out and hold the gear-shift lever in place.

As we left Mogollon, Charlie said the reason for the delay was that they had trouble starting the car that morning. The cars were kept in a garage at the Last Chance Mine, about a half mile out of town. As we were creeping slowly past the mine a fellow stepped on the running board.

"Say," he said to Charlie Marriott, "we put coal oil into your tank this morning instead of gasoline."

No wonder they had trouble starting the motor! There were no filling stations in those days, and gasoline and kerosene were shipped out here in identical fifty-gallon drums. It is easy to see how the error occurred. But there was some gas in the tank; it mixed with the kerosene and after the motor was warmed up we kept rolling. We reached the

Meader station on Big Dry Creek at 12:10; we reached Warm Springs, near Cliff, at 2:15 and had lunch; we got to the Gila post office at 3:40 and there was a short delay in attending to the mail.

NOVEMBER 6, 1907: *Everything went finely till 4:45 when a tire went flat. Busted two tires by 6:45 and, as we were out of them, had to sit and wait for another machine to come out. It came at 9:05.*

At that time the telephone line from Silver City went only as far as Gila, about thirty miles. The driver comforted us when we were finally down for want of tires. Our time of departure had been telephoned ahead and if we did not arrive in town in a reasonable time "they will know something is wrong and send out another car."

As I recall, there was a little snow on the ground and it was a long, dismal wait sitting there in the cold for more than two hours. Finally, towards nine o'clock, we saw headlights showing on a distant hill, then they disappeared, but at last Charlie made the welcome announcement: "There they come now."

When the car was turned around and pointed back toward Silver City we all got in with the mail, leaving those who had brought it to repair the tires and take our old car to town. It was 11:30 when we got to Silver City. I recall that some lodge was initiating a new member by carrying him through the streets in a coffin, a hilarious crowd following it. On the whole, I must have enjoyed that ride. I find the following notation in my diary:

NOVEMBER 6, 1907: *This is an elegant trip to make in an auto and it beats the stage 100 to 1 (?).*

Possibly, that question mark left part of the tale untold.

The following series of entries tells the story of the experiment to carry mail by automobile:

JULY 1, 1907: *Mail was to have come in early as autos were to start today but old stage came out—here at 8:15. New cars made trial run out and drivers were in town at 9 P.M.*

NOVEMBER 2, 1907: *Mail came in on automobile at 7:45—first trip.*

DECEMBER 9, 1907: *Autos have been taken off line indefinitely and stage came out today, getting here at 8:30.*

They COULD depend on the horses in those days!

ROADSIDE DENTAL AND OPTICAL SERVICE

FEBRUARY 2, 1910: *Dr. Mercer, dentist, came on stage at 6:30.*

FEBRUARY 3: *Dentist worked on Mrs. W.'s teeth in A.M. and part of P.M. He also worked on mine after dinner.*

THERE WERE TWO DOCTORS in Mogollon who would attend to the country folks when occasion required, but there was no dentist in the area. However, one came out from Silver City at intervals with his equipment, going here and there where needed. Twice that year he set up at The Oaks, where we were staying, and worked on the teeth of several of us, as well as neighbors who were informed of his presence.

APRIL 22: *A man was here about noon selling specticals.*

Among the traveling salesmen who went from ranch to ranch in those days was an optician. A Japanese cook named Watanabe was employed at The Oaks. About noon on the above date, as I was going home from our office, I saw the traveling optician and Watanabe standing at the side of the road. The Japanese cook had the eye-testing harness across his nose. On a big sycamore tree about twenty feet away was tacked the usual cardboard chart, with a large E at the top and the letters getting smaller and smaller toward the bottom.

Apparently the traveling man got an order. In a week or two I handed Watanabe a small package from our mail sack and later that day he was wearing glasses. We never saw the optician again and Watanabe left the country some thirty-five years ago, but that old sycamore still stands just across the road from the main entrance to The Oaks.

STATEHOOD

SEPTEMBER 5, 1910: *In Cooney I served as clerk of election, appointing delegates to the Territorial convention in Santa Fé Oct. 6 to frame a constitution for the new state.*

AUGUST 21, 1911: *President Taft signed bill today admitting New Mexico as a State!**

I NEVER HAD A VOTE for President of the United States until I was thirty-two years old. In Indiana, in 1900, I lacked a year of being voting age. At the time of the general election of 1904 I was in New Mexico,

---

* This was a resolution admitting New Mexico as a state. The enabling act, or "Statehood Bill," was dated June 20, 1910, and called for the election of delegates to the constitutional convention. This culminated New Mexico's more than fifty-year struggle for statehood, during the course of which more than sixty bills were introduced in Congress.

where we had a vote in Territorial elections but none in the national. I likewise had to pass up the choosing of a President in 1908. But in 1912 New Mexico was a fullfledged state; for the first time, I exercised my privilege to cast a ballot in a national election.

THE "FLU" EPIDEMIC

LIKE NEARLY EVERYWHERE ELSE in the world, Mogollon was hit by the influenza epidemic in the fall of 1918, and hit hard. Whole families were stricken and bedfast. There were two resident physicians in Mogollon, but they were unable to take care of all the sick.

An Army doctor was sent out, also a nurse. On his advice deer were killed to make soup for families unable to provide for themselves, although it was the closed season for hunting. In all, fifty-two people of this community died from influenza, including a top official of one of the mining companies.

Deaths occurred with such frequency that there were not enough able-bodied men in camp to blast out the graves in the hard ground of the local cemetery fast enough to keep up with the fatal cases. The corpses were laid on benches in the old dance hall to await their turn for burial. It was said that cats found their way into that building and gnawed on the faces of the dead—a gruesome thing.

But like other communities, in time the epidemic ran its course and the camp got back into its normal routine.

GLENWOOD

EARLIER I WROTE THAT WHAT IS NOW GLENWOOD was formerly called Whitewater, after the creek on which it was located. For a number of years before the growth of the community at its present site, the post office for that part of the country was at a little settlement on Whitewater Creek about five miles above where Glenwood is now located. This was Graham.

Graham was established because a mill was constructed there for treating gold and silver ore from the Confidence Mine, which was located several miles on up in the mountains. A pipeline up Whitewater Creek furnished water power for the milling operation. Ore was hauled down to the mill by wagon; part of the present road to Mogollon was originally constructed for that purpose. There were houses for employees and, of course, a store. The project was abandoned more than forty-five years ago and the village soon vanished; only a tailing pile and remnants of the old mill remain. The old townsite is now known as Graham Park and has facilities for picnicking. A little above it is the Cat Walk, a great tourist attraction.

According to Post Office Department records, the name of the post office at Graham was changed to Clear Creek on October 1, 1904. The name was again changed to Glenwood on September 11, 1906, "at which time its [the post office's] site was moved five miles." Thus the present Glenwood.

The constricted valley of Whitewater Creek narrows to an abrupt end at Graham Park. Sheer, towering walls form a gorge which is only a few feet wide in places. With water always in the creek at this point, it made passage difficult through a few hundred feet of the canyon. Sometime during the 1930's, as a Civilian Conservation Corps project, a walkway was constructed through this portion. It became known as the Cat Walk.

Cables were anchored to the high rock walls to support a narrow, eyebrow-like wooden walk, with railing, which winds around the face of the cliff some twenty-five feet above the stream. It is thrilling to make a trip over that walk on a warm summer day with the gin-clear water murmuring among the rocks below. If you are quick-eyed you'll see a trout darting here and there in one of the pools, and there is always a cool breeze through the shaded canyon.

In 1904 there were only three residences in the immediate vicinity of Glenwood: George Rowe operated the stage station at the site of the Los Olmos Guest Ranch; Ernest Kitt lived in "Juniper Cottage," now the home of John Allred; and Lige Sipe had gardens just south of Whitewater Creek at the place now occupied by Whitewater Lodge. Sipe delivered fruit and vegetables to the mining camps until he was murdered in 1909.

Over the years Glenwood has developed into a delightful village with several business establishments, tourist accommodations, two swimming pools, and numerous residences. With its remarkable setting among immense cottonwoods, the place is like an oasis. Located on US 260, the "Park-to-Park Highway" between Carlsbad Caverns and the Grand Canyon, it is easy of access. Many week-end tourists and vacationers make it their headquarters for visiting nearby historic areas and ghost towns or packing into the unspoiled wilderness of the Gila National Forest.

II

Days of Death and Violence

Posse Gathering at Cooney, New Mexico

View from the Little Fanney Mine

SOME TALES OF INDIAN DAYS

AMONG MY EARLY ACQUAINTANCES in Cooney was George Doyle, who was what I now think of as a typical, legendary prospector and miner. He had been in these mountains many years.

In a reminiscent mood one day, Doyle told me of an Indian raid on Cooney in the early 80's. The camp had been alerted by runners from Clairmont, a settlement two or three miles north: The Indians were en route to Cooney. The residents took to the mountain sides, and the camp was soon evacuated. Doyle said that he and another miner, John Lambert, hid among some bushes on a hillside to the south. They had a little dog with them. When the Indians came into view, filing down the canyon, the dog began to growl. The miners were afraid it might bark and disclose their presence; they choked it to death on the spot.

When the party reached the village they ransacked the dwellings. Doyle saw a squaw come out of one house with a large mirror hung down her back. The children were in great glee and jostled each other for a peek into it—perhaps the first time those little shavers ever had a look at themselves. The visitors finally left and the residents returned to their homes.

The late M. E. Coates told me of the killing of Sergeant James C. Cooney on April 29, 1880. Mr. Coates was a resident of Alma when I came to the country; he later operated a store in Mogollon. He was in the "siege of Alma," when all the local residents were huddled into a log cabin.

The Indians came in the night, but did not molest them then. At break of day, one of the party, Wilcox, opened the door slightly for a look. He was killed immediately by a bullet in his forehead. There may have been other shots; I do not recall all that was told me. But finally the Indians left and went on up Mineral Creek towards Camp Cooney. Still later, Sergeant Cooney decided to ride up that way and reconnoiter. A few hours afterwards his horse came back, riderless.

The next morning a posse went up the creek and found the sergeant's mutilated body near where it is now interred. Miners blasted a hole in an immense boulder, deposited the body and sealed it up. Today the site is fenced and known as the "Cooney Tomb." Sergeant Cooney located the first mine in this district.*

---

* In 1870 Sergeant James C. Cooney was stationed at Fort Bayard, in command of a detachment which was mapping the area. While on a scouting trip he located a rich gold deposit on Mineral Creek. He kept the discovery a secret until his enlistment was over; then, in 1876, he returned to work the deposit.

In July, 1908, I married a local girl whose parents came from Scotland. Her father had died about thirty days before I arrived in Cooney. Years later her mother told me that some time in the 80's they were traveling in a covered wagon in the Tularosa country, some sixty miles north of here, when it was rumored that the Apaches were again on the loose. When they came to the foot of a long, steep hill they stopped and her husband decided to walk to the top for a look. Before leaving he handed her the six-shooter from his belt and told her that should the Indians come while he was gone she should first shoot the children, then herself. He took his rifle and walked to the top. Fortunately, nothing happened.

In this era of easy, rapid transport, without thought of roadside ambush, it is a bit difficult to realize that such traveling conditions could have existed so recently.

A KANGAROO COURT IN COONEY

AUGUST 10, 1905: *Bearup killed Lee Taylor this evening.*

THAT WAS THE LAST ENTRY in my diary for the day. That was D. E. Bearup who, with his family, lived at the foot of the mountain about two miles below Mogollon where he conducted a small mining operation, sometimes hiring a man or two.

On August 11th a "court" was convened in Cooney in a miner's cabin; Dan Higgins, Justice of the Peace, was judge. C. H. Kirkpatrick, at one time a United States Commissioner, represented the Territory (we did not get statehood until years later). A man named Frank McGinn, a bookkeeper for the M G & C Co. in Cooney who had studied law, was attorney for the defense.

Crowd came about 10 and held trial. . . . They fooled along until about noon and adjourned trial till 1 o'clock. . . . Trial drug along, taking testimony, until nearly six. They adjourned until 9 A.M. tomorrow.

I was there at intervals that day until 4:30, when I left after listening a while to McGinn's plea for the defendant. While the proceedings were conducted with judicial dignity, the physical surroundings could easily have suggested a "Kangaroo Court." I remember at one of the hearings a fellow came in and sat on the bed with several coils of rope hanging on his arm—a Smart-Aleck suggestion. It was a small, one-roomed cabin. The judge presided behind a little kitchen table. There was a chair or two and a bench, as I recall. I along with several others sat on the side of the bed while still others leaned against the walls.

Just what the judge's decision was I do not remember, but the defendant was likely bound over to the district court, for on September 11 I have this notation: *Bearup came back from Socorro today.* Socorro was then our countyseat.

Bearup eventually got out of it, but we understood at the time that it cost him a considerable sum. Soon after the shooting my friend Tom Cooney told me that as he was coming up-trail below Mogollon the afternoon of the shooting he had met Taylor going down. Taylor "had been drinking." After chatting a moment as he started to leave Taylor told Cooney, "I'm going down and kill old man Bearup." Instead, he was the victim.

Tom was busy and said he did not want "to be bothered" going over to Cooney and testifying at the trial. But had he done so frontier justice would likely have exonerated Mr. Bearup at the preliminary hearing.

THE FREEMAN-CLARK MURDER

FEBRUARY 19, 1912: *About 8 o'clock Walter Jones and John Allred called and told me that C. A. Freeman and Billy Clark were killed this evening, and store safe robbed by two Mexicans. This is terrible.*

WE WERE LIVING about a half a mile above Alma at the time. There was a knock at the door, and I was surprised to see my neighbors, each with a rifle in his hand. They told me of the holdup of the Mogollon Mercantile store in Mogollon and of the killing of Freeman and Clark. The road past my place was one of only two out of the country at that time. Jones and Allred wanted to stand in my yard and try to get the bandits should they come that way. But their trail was picked up later and it led through the heart of the rugged Mogollon mountains; that it was followed some thirty miles through such terrain always seemed to me a superb piece of trailing.

The only others in the store at the time were "Red" Burns, the cashier, and two clerks. Clark had been a bystander who was in the center of the room. He was shot through the heart by one of the bandits and died immediately. Freeman was the manager. He was standing outside of the counter. The other man shot him in the neck; he sank slowly to the floor and was soon dead.

Red said he "expected to get it next." One of the men pointed to the safe with the barrel of his gun. He was told that it was not locked. The two then helped themselves and fled. Red then went to the Sil Gamblin bar across the street and reported what had just taken place. It was a very windy night. Men in the barroom had heard the shots but thought it was the wind slamming the shutters. When Red got there someone got busy on the telephone.

The post office at that time was in the rear of the Coates & Moore store, two doors below the Mogollon Mercantile place. It was common knowledge that the bank in Silver City usually mailed a package of money about the 19th of the month to cash payroll checks on the 20th. Soon after arrival of the stage the mail was taken from the post office to the other store, and a few minutes later those two men entered. They had undoubtedly been in the shadows watching for the opportune moment to effect the robbery.

FEBRUARY 22: *Heard that posses are on trail of murderers of Freeman and Clark.*

FEBRUARY 23: *Home at 5:15. Went to Alma. The Freeman-Clark murderers were taken on the Gila, while I was in Alma— one was shot and the other taken alive—had $2000.00 on them.*

In due time "the other" was hung in Socorro, our county seat.

SOME OTHER KILLINGS—ILLEGAL and OTHERWISE

Trouble With the Law

AUGUST 28, 1910: . . . *learned that Chas. Clark died in Silver City today.*

FOR SOME TIME before the stage holdup on August 9, 1910, when the driver was killed and the bullion taken off, high-grading and lawlessness had become so flagrant that two Territorial Mounted Policemen had been sent to Mogollon, there being a strong suspicion that the local officers were a little too indifferent to what was going on. Later one of the Mounted Police arrested a man without a warrant, thinking he had a gun—he had none.

This and other events aroused the antagonism of the community to the point that a warrant was issued by the Justice of the Peace here for the arrest of one of the Territorial men. But upon being served with it, he refused to recognize the local officer, a Charles Clark who was also a local saloon keeper.

AUGUST 27: *Stage driver brought word up that Chas. Clark was seriously if not fatally shot last night at Mogollon by one of the Mounted Police . . . heard Clark was taken to Silver City Hospital.*

Clark died the next day. He was buried on August 30th behind the Cooney Tomb on Mineral Creek.

Versions have differed as to just what occurred on the night of August 26th, but the account as related by E. D. McIntosh,* who was on the scene, should be authentic:

> . . . the cause of so much anger and lust for revenge among the town people was due to the manner in which Clark was killed. He was given a warrant to serve on P— and went behind his bar and picked up his Winchester. This was about 8 o'clock that night. P— climbed up on an oil drum outside the window and, looking down above the glazed [opaque] lower half, he was within ten or twelve feet of Clark and he shot him.
>
> The next morning someone phoned from the mine office that B— and P— were coming down, so the people were armed and waiting. When they rode into town George Williams came into our store with a Winchester and said there was someone with a gun behind every window and door on the opposite side of the street and that Mr. Freeman and I were delegated to go down and try to get the officers to

---

* E. D. McIntosh was a resident of the Mogollon area during his youth. He was in the grocery business in Alaska during the gold rush there and returned to Mogollon in 1906. He built a general merchandise store which he operated until the early 1920's when he sold out and moved to a farm near Las Cruces.

disarm. They tied their horses in front of Coates & Moore, and Freeman and I walked down and explained the situation to them and asked them to give up their guns. I'll never forget the reply:

"If you guys want a fight, just turn your dogs loose."

Boy, what a situation. We knew that Rass Perry and a couple of others were in the Holland Building watching and with a desire to shoot, and that the saloons had men armed and watching, but what made my hair stand out was the knowledge that Irvin Moore was behind the fence between Holland's and Sil Gamblin's with a shot gun loaded with buck shot. Just when things were about to come to pass, Mr. Brooks, a U. S. Cattle Inspector, rode up and tied his horse and joined us, thinking nothing was amiss. Freeman and I explained the situation and advised that he take the two officers with him and leave town, which he did and which I think was the wise thing to do; although most people called Clark's death a cold-blooded murder, P— was acquitted at his trial in Socorro. That is the story as it really happened.

There was no question about the shooting having taken place from outside the building, for that neat, round hole was in that window for a long time before the pane was replaced. This was in the old Jimmie Johnson bar, in downtown Mogollon.

Many years afterward the late Ira Gregory, an old-timer then, told me he was standing behind the open door of Sil Gamblin's bar, thirty feet away, with a cocked 30-30 at his shoulder, the muzzle at the crack

Election Day in Cooney — November, 1904.

ready for instant action, while the parley with the Mounted Police was going on.

About a year and a half later Mr. Freeman who with E. D. McIntosh parleyed with the officers that day was himself the victim of a tragic event in Mogollon, as we have seen.

Those Mounted Police left the community, which soon settled back into its routine of running mines, stores, bars and home affairs. There was a change of local officers and not much happened—for a while.

"A Good Man When Sober, But —"

DURING THE PERIOD of these reminiscences one of the saloon operators in Mogollon was Pete Almarez, who was also more or less of a professional gambler. About 6 o'clock on the morning of March 16, 1907, as he was going toward his home in the upper part of town after his night's work, he became aware of a Mexican following him. As Pete glanced behind him, the man was just reaching for his hip pocket. Thinking he was about to pull a gun, Pete quickly drew his own and shot the fellow through the heart.

It was found later that the dead man had only a pocketful of rocks and was, presumably, about to use them. That evening I called at the cabin where he was laid out on a couple of planks, a tall candle alight at head and foot. The attendant opened his shirt and pointed out for me the bullet hole in his breast.

Almost exactly ten years later Pete Almarez again cropped up in my diary:

MARCH 21, 1917: *Pete Almarez killed saloonman Zapata in Mogollon this evening.*

I was then living near Alma. Only recently did I learn what was behind this affair. E. D. McIntosh told me about the killing:

One of the characters in the camp who was really bad when he was drinking was Pedro Almarez. There was bitter feeling between him and Cosme Zapata. . . . Zapata ran a saloon down at lower end of the sidewalk below Coates & Moore and when one of them was drunk he would look up the other one for a fight. One night Cosme came into Pete's saloon and walked up to the bar with a double action pistol in his hand. Pete saw what was coming. He was sober and had his gun in his hand, and when Cosme put his hands on the bar Pete was there with his gun cocked. Pete watched Cosme's hammer and told him not to pull it back any farther. They stood there several moments and Cosme pulled the hammer back a little and Pete shot him.

I do not think any charges were ever brought against Almarez for either of these killings, but a few years later he, too, died with his boots on.

Pete was very drunk one day, about 1920 or '21, and went over to George Williams' saloon.* George was alone at the time and Pete backed him into a corner with his gun and told George he was going to kill him. George really used his head then and told Pete that he was not afraid to die, but his wife and children would be destitute as he had not made a will and asked for a little time to make one. After some argument and some soft talk by George, Pete said "all right, but just one hour." He would be back in an hour and kill him. George sent word to Bill Clark, the deputy.† Bill, with a double barreled shot gun went to the door of Pete's saloon and kicked it open. Pete was standing behind his bar and started to move over toward his gun when Bill told him to come out from behind the bar and not to move toward his gun or he would shoot. Pete stood for a moment, then made a move to his right when Bill let him have both barrels. A man sitting there said that Pete's shirt ballooned out like a tent—and that was the last of Pete Almarez, a good man when sober but very bad when drunk.

I recall one further detail: When Pete's gun was examined it was not loaded!

"Just Passing Events"

OCTOBER 22, 1909: *Heard this morning that Sterling Ashby killed Lige Sipe yesterday evening at 7 o'clock at the W-S ranch, by stabbing.*

Sipe was a former resident of Glenwood and Ashby lived near Alma. He eventually served a long term at Santa Fe. Upon his release in the early '20's he returned to Alma and later went to Arizona, where he was employed as a night watchman by a group of businessmen. One night, when trying to intercept the holdup of a filling station, he was shot through the neck by one of the robbers, ending his life.

❊   ❊   ❊

In late 1914 and early '15 a man named John W. Davis did some assessment work for us. Later he was employed by one of the other mining companies near Mogollon. At a drinking party one night he got into a quarrel with a local blacksmith. Later, when outside, Davis slipped up behind the man and split his head open with a hatchet. Davis was taken to Socorro and jailed. Word came back that he had

---

* During the Prohibition Era most of the saloons in Mogollon remained in business. They had their pool tables, card games, and dispensed soft drinks. There may also have been some traffic in "untaxed" goods, "under the counter," with their old, reliable customers.

† The Charles Clark who was killed by a Territorial Policeman was the father of Bill Clark who, as a deputy sheriff, killed Pete Almarez. The Billy Clark who was murdered in the holdup of the Mogollon Mercantile Company store on February 19, 1912, was from Cornwall, England, and no kin to the other two Clarks.

crushed the light bulb in his cell, swallowed the glass, and died from it. The county was thus spared the cost of a trial.

❧ ❧ ❧

During the period of heavy shipments of material from Silver City to Mogollon in 1908 and '09, among the many freighters was a man named Hightower. On delivery of freight to the mine these individual haulers would bring their okayed waybills to the office and get a check for the load. A time or two Hightower's wife came to the window with him. He was a tall, rather slender man with a big, blond handlebar mustache; his wife was a short, plump, pleasant-faced woman. A few years later they lived in a tent at Tyrone, ten miles west of Silver City.

One night, in a drunken rage, her husband killed her with a shotgun blast. He was duly arrested, tried, and sentenced to be hung. In those days a man was executed in the county in which the crime was committed, and for this purpose a scaffold was erected back of the old Silver City courthouse. At the hanging, when Hightower went through the trap his head was jerked off. My friend Tom Cooney was there at the time; although he did not witness the execution, he was in the rear of the courthouse when the sheriff brought the man's head in and put it in a sink under a faucet.

"It was a bloody mess," Tom told me.

FEBRUARY 11, 1911: *Heard today that Jim Vickery was shot yesterday, probably fatally.*

For some time prior to that date Vickery operated a slaughter house about five miles out of Mogollon, not far off the road to Glenwood. He supplied fresh meat to the local butcher shops. The driver of a car en route to Mogollon had seen Vickery sitting at the side of the road, in a bloody condition; he had been shot through the chest. The motorist took him to town where there were two doctors.

Vickery would never tell who shot him, remarking that when he got well he would take care of the man himself. He seemed to be making satisfactory progress toward recovery, but it was not to be.

FEBRUARY 17, 1911: *Heard that Jim Vickery died at 9:30 last night, from being shot a week ago.*

He died suddenly, the doctors thought from a blood clot on the brain as a result of the injury. . . . Thus the secret of Vickery's assailant died with him.

❧ ❧ ❧

OCTOBER 8, 1911: *A Negro killed a Mexican in Mogollon last night.*

MAY 30, 1912: *Red Simmons was buried today—died yesterday—was shot last Saturday (25th) by Baca.*

While at first glance it may seem that Mogollon was pretty lawless in those days, these sundry "killings" were not very close together, and we were inclined to look upon them as just passing events. Most of the residents were ordinary, peaceful folks and did not think of the community as being anything out of the ordinary. It certainly was not as bad as some of the earlier mining camps of the Far West. An elderly ex-resident of one of them who operated a boarding house told me: "We had a man for breakfast every morning."

THE HOLLIMON-HANNIGAN AFFAIR

FEBRUARY 16, 1906: *Bob Hollimon held up stage and took Hannigan off this morning.*

FEBRUARY 19: *Heard that Bob Hollimon got $1000.00 out of Hannigan and let him go.*

THIS WAS THE PRELUDE to an unusual drama which was enacted here. I had only a few details of it then and just recently got more specific information of the event from one who played an unwonted but somewhat benevolent part in the affair—Louis Jones who, with his brother Walter, then operated a store in Alma known as Jones Bros.

I knew Bob Hollimon quite well during my earlier years here. He was a quiet, soft-voiced, gentlemanly and very likeable person. Yet, there was something about his makeup that bespoke caution. Captain William French in his book, *Some Recollections of a Western Ranchman,* paid eloquent tribute to him in that respect. He was the type that once aroused, Hell goes to popping.

Hannigan had a cattle ranch west of Alma. Bob worked for him and had been promised a percentage of the calves branded. Finally Hannigan sold out, and without making any arrangements for a settlement with Hollimon; it appeared he was about to leave the country.

The stage left Mogollon after midnight in those days and likely got out of Glenwood before daylight that time of year. In the early morning of February 16, 1906, on that first hill below Glenwood, Bob stopped the stage and at gun's point made Hannigan get out. The stage then proceeded, unmolested. To prevent easy tracking, Bob wrapped gunny sacks around Hannigan's feet and then marched him to the Little Whitewater country east of Glenwood. He then took a chain and padlocked Hannigan to a tree.

The chain was long enough to reach a small stream; there was a cup so he could get a drink. For food a bag of hard sourdough biscuits was left within reach. During February it can get pretty cold in those foothills. Fortunately Hannigan had on a heavy overcoat. He and Bob must have had some sort of a settlement then and there, for Bob rode over to Alma with an order from Hannigan to pay him $1000.

The Jones Bros. had $600 cash in their store. Then by some rustling during the next two days they raised a hundred here and another there from among ranchers in the country until the $1000 was in hand and paid to Bob. He then went back over to the Little Whitewater, leading a saddle horse and accompanied by two men, unchained Hannigan and brought him to Louis Jones' house at Alma.

They arrived about mid-forenoon. Hannigan was a large, elderly man, and his condition was "pitiful" after being chained up for three nights. They fed him soup and put him to bed. "He slept solidly until eleven the next morning," Jones said. Hannigan admitted owing the money and "intended to pay him later." But Bob struck before the iron started to cool off!

Hannigan then had a son who was running a saloon in Deming. He wrote him and in a few days the boy sent $1000 to his father in Alma. Those who had put up the money were reimbursed. During all that time Hannigan was staying with Louis Jones and his family. When it was over Hannigan did not offer to pay anything; he didn't even thank them for their courtesies.

The "law" made but token efforts to apprehend Bob, it being generally understood that Hannigan "had it coming to him." Hollimon's nephew, the late Fred Hollimon of Alma, a boy at the time, said his uncle "got away on the best horse in the country, which is the same as getting out today in a Cadillac." He went to California, where he resided unmolested many years.

WILLIAM McGINNIS: TRAIN ROBBER

DECEMBER 25, 1905: *Saw McGinnis, just out of the "pen"—an ex-train robber. Seems like a decent fellow.*

DURING THE LATE 90's, the WS ranch, near Alma, had the dubious distinction of serving as a base of operations for Butch Cassidy and several members of his infamous Wild Bunch. Like so many bad things that came to this part of the country, their coming brought some good to somebody. In this case, a great deal of money came to Alma and a beleaguered rancher found relief from cattle rustling.

Captain William French, a Britisher who operated the WS ranch at that time, hired some of these outlaws without knowledge of their identity. Prior to their advent on the range, Captain French had many difficulties—cattle rustling, false branding of his calves, and the like. After hiring one Jim Lowe to take charge of operations, and after Jim Lowe hired other of his friends, the depredations practically ceased.

Jim Lowe eventually proved to be the notorious Butch Cassidy, leader of the Wild Bunch; another was wanted over a wide area of the West under the name of Elza Lay. Captain French described him as "much taller and darker—in fact a quite good-looking young man, debonair, with a bit of a swagger. He seemed quite a cut above the ordinary cow hand and undoubtedly had more education. He owned up to the name of 'William McGinnis'."*

After a considerable period of very satisfactory service by the new WS employees, Mac (as McGinnis was called) decided to quit, but requested that he be permitted to accompany a train shipment of cattle to a new pasture in Colfax County in the northeastern part of the territory, to which French agreed. A little later the captain arrived up there, and in a day or two learned that a train on the Colorado Southern had been held up near Folsom, New Mexico. That did not distract him until he was told someone had recognized one of the bandits as having been employed by the WS ranch. That startled Captain French. He wrote, "That Mac, a paladin amongst cow-punchers, should stoop to train robbing was unthinkable."

After the holdup three bandits took to the hills on their horses and headed for Cimarron Canyon. A posse of eight or ten men got on their trail and came upon the trio in their camp the next day. On the first volley from the officers two of the robbers were wounded, but they took cover and returned the fire with such intensity that three of the posse were killed and several injured. That "paladin amongst cow-punchers" was eventually captured after being recognized from widely-published pictures.

He refused to own to the name Elza Lay and was tried for murder as William K. McGinnis. The penalty for murder or train robbery was death; the fact that Mac got off with a life sentence is attributed to his engaging personality. The jury recommended mercy. "On October 10, 1899, [he was] sentenced to serve a term of life for murder from Colfax County, New Mexico. The record further indicates that he was

---

* French devoted the last two chapters of his book, *Some Recollections of a Western Ranchman, New Mexico 1883-1899* (New York, Frederick A. Stokes Company), to his experiences with members of the Wild Bunch.

WILLIAM H. ANTRIM, *the stepfather of Billy the Kid, was a resident of the Mogollons and was well known to the author. "I was intimately acquainted with Uncle Billy Antrim, as he was called, and during all those years I do not recall his ever having mentioned Billy the Kid to me," said Mr. Hoover.*

The above picture of Antrim, center, was taken at the portal of the Confidence Mine tunnel, near Mogollon, in the 1890's.

discharged January 10, 1906," according to official Penitentiary of New Mexico records.

Indeed his personality must have been engaging! While that discharge date may have been officially set for January 10th, McGinnis was actually set free about three weeks earlier, perhaps as a holiday gesture to let him spend Christmas with his friends around Alma where he worked for several years. I recall that at the time it was said the warden of the penitentiary would, on occasion, take McGinnis buggy riding around Santa Fé. Prison records throw no light on the subject: "We regret that we are unable to furnish you with further information, due to the fact that we are unable to locate a file for McGinnis. Whether or not a file was made, or whether it has been misplaced, is not known to this office."

On Christmas day, 1905, the Alma community held the usual festivities of the season, among them cowpony races, which I attended. Thus the entry in my diary about William McGinnis. It was the only time I ever saw him, and it was the first time I had heard of him. That day he seemed to be the main attraction among both men and women. To me, a tenderfoot at the time, it was hard to believe that a man with such gentlemanly demeanor could have undertaken the hazardous job of holding up a train. Sometimes I feel inclined to take off my hat to one with that kind of guts. Had he gotten into the right channel he might have gone far in legitimate business.

After his release from prison McGinnis stayed in Alma for about a year and a half. He stayed with Louis and Walter Jones, who had a general merchandise store. "He seemed to trust us," Louis Jones told me.* Finally he bought a good saddle horse and one day remarked that he knew where there was a cache of money in a box, "buried under the root of a juniper tree on the Mexican border." He told the Jones brothers he would be gone two weeks, and if he was not back by then they "would know something had happened" to him. He returned in thirteen days with $58,000 "wrapped in a slicker on the back of his saddle." That money was dumped in the corner of a utility room behind a small bar that adjoined the store and covered with gunny sacks. It remained there until Mac left Alma.

Among the money was about $1100 in silver. When they needed "change" in the store, one of them would hand Mac some currency and he would bring them a like amount in silver. Eventually the silver was exhausted.

* Louis Jones was reluctant to have the story released, but finally remarked "It was so long ago—"

The money did not come from the Folsom train robbery. It is a matter of record that the express messenger had hastily removed the valuables from the safe and hid them in another part of the car and then spun the knob on the safe. When the gang blasted it open, it was empty. More likely it came from a train holdup at Grants, New Mexico, October 8, 1897. A hundred thousand dollars was taken; none was recovered, no one was caught, and the methods had the stamp of a Wild Bunch operation.*

For several months before Mac left on his trip to recover that money he sent letters to first one and then another of his former accomplices. One by one, the letters came back, "unclaimed," so he finally decided to go after it himself. After returning, he stayed around Alma for several months. Finally he left for Wyoming with the money tied on his saddle. The Jones brothers corresponded with him for several years. He wrote them that he had invested $40,000 in a cattle ranch and was "going straight" from then on. Eventually his letters ceased, and it was never heard what may have become of William McGinnis.

THE KILLING OF RALPH JENKS

IT WAS NOT LONG after my arrival here in 1904 when I began to hear of the "Jenks Cabins" as landmarks in these mountains. The family, with three boys, Bill, Ralph and Roy, lived in Mogollon three or four years during the 1890's. Later they built a cabin on Silver Creek several miles above Mogollon. Still later, they moved across the range and built a cabin on Willow Creek. Eventually another Jenks Cabin appeared still farther down that creek. Finally the family moved to West Fork, in the heart of what is now the Gila Wilderness, where they constructed a much larger house. In later years this cabin was acquired by the State Game Department and used as a fish hatchery until the present modern hatchery was built at Glenwood.

The Jenks boys had acquired a few cattle and ranged them in that area. In the summer of 1900 some cattle had been stolen from northern Grant County and there was much suspicion that these boys were implicated. Deputy Sheriff W. D. "Keechi" Johnson was given a warrant to inspect the Jenks' cattle and make any necessary arrests. In August he proceeded, alone, to the Jenks cabin on West Fork to make that inspection.

Since the range was a number of miles away, a pack horse and camping equipment were provided at the Jenks home. The officer and Ralph then left for the grazing area. From subsequent information, soon after

---

* See J. Wesley Huff, "Malpais Mystery," *New Mexico*, XXV (April, 1947), p. 35 ff.

Ben Lilly, the Lion Hunter, and Four Friends

they left, Roy Jenks, Ralph's brother, took a roundabout trail to a point where he knew they would have to pass and, by fast riding, was there upon their arrival. He shot and killed the deputy. Later, in a letter to the *Silver City Independent*, Ralph wrote that he did not know who did the shooting:

> . . . I then started for Mogollon to notify the sheriff there of what had occurred, and met my youngest brother at Willow Creek and had him do it for me. Mr. Foster, Mr. Murray and Mr. Kerr, justice of the peace, came out at once and a coroner's jury was collected, my testimony heard, and after the verdict we buried Mr. Johnson.

As the evidence looked bad for Ralph Jenks, he was later arrested and taken into custody in Mogollon, along with a man named Henry Reinhardt, who was also believed involved.

J. Marvin Hunter, Sr., of Bandera, Texas, one of the deputy officers who took those men to Silver City, has written: "We had left Mogollon about 9 o'clock that morning with Jenks and Reinhardt in tow, and after we got over the mountain and hit the arroyos, we averaged about five miles an hour. We must have been about fifty miles from Mogollon when the tragedy occurred." The tragedy took place when Jenks allegedly pulled a gun* from the saddle scabbard of Deputy Edgar Scarborough, who then drew his pistol and killed the man. Continuing Mr. Hunter's letter: "This delayed us probably an hour or more."

Jenks' body was covered with a tarp, weighted down with rocks around the edges, and left by the side of the road. "We started for Silver City about 10:30, travelled until after twelve o'clock, and as our horses were pretty well jaded, we camped until daylight and got up and proceeded on our way. We reached Silver City around noon. District court was in session, Scarborough was placed in jail, and the case was immediately considered by the grand jury, which no-billed Scarborough. I heard the District Judge tell Sheriff Blair to take some men and go out and bury Jenks. . . . I always held to the idea that they buried him where he fell, but of this I am not certain."

There are different versions among the old-timers here of just what occurred. One is that Jenks, with "his hands tied behind his back on a horse," was deliberately shot, "a cold-blooded murder." This is denied by Mr. Hunter. Another version is that Jenks was wearing "heavy canvas gloves" and with that handicap could not have been manipulating the gun claimed to have been pulled from Scarborough's scabbard. After the killing, Scarborough was placed under arrest by the senior officer of the party; this and the fact that he was placed in the Silver City jail suggests that there was something irregular in the killing.

---

* Some versions say it was a shotgun. Hunter identified the weapon as a 30-40 Krag-Jorgensen.

At that time H. J. "Bill" Evans and his wife Nina lived on a homestead in the forest about three miles above Mogollon. Mrs. Evans was a large, frontier-type woman, seemingly more masculine than feminine, and able to take care of herself in any situation. They were friends of the Jenks family. Local tradition has it that after this affair Roy Jenks, the actual murderer of officer Johnson, was hidden in the forest near the Evans home by her while she made a set of false whiskers which he wore while getting out of the country.

Soon after, the remainder of the family left for parts unknown. But the so-called Jenks Cabins will remain as landmarks in the Mogollons for a long time to come.

ANOTHER STAGE HOLDUP

DECEMBER 19, 1912: *Mogollon stage was held up last night by Whitie and others and they were captured.*

IN THE SUMMER OF 1908 among the newcomers to Mogollon was a man named White—I forget his initials. Everybody simply called him "Whitie." He was rather small of stature and a natural clown; he might have made a good actor. But his greatest attribute was uncontrolled laughter from hardly any cause at all. It was not a chuckle, but a loud, deep belly laugh that could he heard a long way. His main trade was blacksmithing, but he was handy in other ways, too.

Some time after my wife and I returned from our wedding trip in August, 1908, Whitie papered the rooms of our house here at the mine and did a fine job of it. I do not recall just what occupations the man followed around here during the next few years, but in 1912 he moved to Glenwood and opened a blacksmith shop just across the road from the upper entrance to what is now the Los Olmos Guest Ranch.

In the latter part of that year he and a man named Jim Harris told Tom Gallagher, the stage driver between Glenwood and Mogollon whom they knew well, that they were going to hold him up on the mountain and for him to give them the mail pouch and he would not be hurt.

Gallagher told George Williams, the postmaster in Mogollon, about it and asked him what to do. George told Gallagher to go right along with them, then he notified the bank officials in Silver City and had them send some State Rangers to be in Mogollon and Glenwood at the time the payroll money would be coming out, December 18th.

As my diary indicates, the holdup came off on schedule. Later I learned that it was actually a singlehanded job. White had stopped the stage in a narrow lane just above Los Olmos, near Glenwood.

As he told it later, he took what he wanted from the registered mail pouch, went back, and hid the package in ashes in his blacksmith shop. Then he went down to the village where a card game was under way. Instead of being in his usual jovial mood, wanting to "sit in," Whitie seemed aloof; he left in a moment, and the brief visit to the village was undoubtedly to provide an alibi.

Presumably he then hastened to his blacksmith shop to inspect his fortune. It would have been worth a pretty penny to have seen the expression on his face when he opened that fat registered package from the bank and found that it contained only a lot of blank paper! I wonder if he let out a booming *Haw! Haw! Haw!* when he realized whom the joke was on.

Jim Harris was a small-scale rancher living west of Alma. I once helped circulate a petition to have him made a peace officer in Mogollon. Later he got the appointment and was holding that office at the time of this affair. The Rangers, knowing of his complicity in this holdup, arrested him in Mogollon that evening. Whitie was taken into custody in Glenwood that night, and the Rangers here reported the arrests to Silver City. Both men were "sent up."

MARCH 8, 1917: (At Alma) *Saw Jim Harris and "Whitie" recently back from Levenworth Pen.*

APRIL 20: *Played 10 games* [of] *freeze-out with Whitie and others.*

Later Whitie, and Harris and his family left the country. I never heard of them again.

Long before the date of those last entries, in my imagination I could now and then hear Whitie's booming laughter at the Sunday ball games, drowning out all other commotion. I like to think that when Whitie came before his Final Judge he was given the benefit of many a doubt just because of his proclivity for unrestrained laughter upon the slightest provocation.

BEN LILLY: LION HUNTER

MANY TIMES I saw him around Alma. I remember him in particular by his long cleft beard. To me, he was just another man until the Alma postmaster told me one day that Ben Lilly "corresponds with Teddy Roosevelt." That gave him some stature in my estimation.

Ben Lilly had long been a professional hunter. He had served as a guide for Theodore Roosevelt on a bear hunting expedition in Louisiana during 1907. In later years Lilly came to New Mexico and for a long while occupied himself principally with hunting mountain lions. For some three years—about 1913, '14 and '15—he hunted the country adjacent to Alma and bought his camp supplies there.

During the period he worked out of Alma he killed 110 lions. The cattlemen there had made up a pot, handled by Louis Jones, the storekeeper, out of which $50 was paid for each lion hide brought in by Lilly. Mr. Jones recalls an incident in that arrangement.

One day Ben killed a female lion and upon cutting her open found two cubs "haired out" and "to be born soon." Lilly skinned them and brought in the hides. "They were about ten inches long and three wide," and Ben thought he should be paid for them too. As Louis would not take it upon himself to do so, he put the matter up to some of the cowmen, several of whom declined payment. Then he saw Hugh McKeen, the largest individual cattleowner at that time. McKeen said that if the lion had not been killed there would have been two more, and he was willing to pay his part. The others then agreed. "So Ben got $150 for that lion." During the three-year period Louis Jones paid Lilly a total of $5500.

I don't know just when Lilly left Alma, as I left there in the spring of 1918 and spent the next ten years in El Paso. However, by around 1930 age had apparently overtaken the old hunter; when I heard of him again he was in the Mary Hines Home for elderly people, on Big Dry Creek, some fifteen miles below Glenwood. Towards the last his mind became affected and he would wander away from the home. Joe Saunders, of Glenwood, who worked for the Mary Hines Home for several years, told me that he "trailed Ben many times through the hills and brought him back."

According to the Certificate of Death, Ben V. Lilly was born in Louisville, Kentucky, in 1844.* He died in Grant County, New Mexico, December 17, 1936, and was buried in Silver City, December 21. His occupation was given as "game hunter."

Thus ended a unique character: A man who abandoned his family to spend his life hunting in remote areas. Many tales have been told about him. He was deeply religious, and if on a hot lion trail on a Saturday evening would abandon it until Monday morning. He would write a check on a cigarette paper, or on a slab of wood whittled thin and smooth. These checks were not always cashed; they were unusual souvenirs from an unusual man.

---

* There is considerable conflict of testimony about the birth of Ben Lilly. The family Bible said he was born December 31, 1856, in Wilcox County, Alabama. For a biography of Ben Lilly, see J. Frank Dobie, *The Ben Lilly Legend*, New York, 1950.

The Author on Whitewater Mesa, October, 1956

Today in the Mogollons*

MUCH WATER has passed over the proverbial dam since April, 1904, when I arrived in the Territory of New Mexico. Cooney, then a picturesque and thriving little mining camp set in a deep gash in the mountain, has since then been almost completely obliterated by fire, flood and the hand of man. Only an occasional retaining wall at the foot of the mountain and the faint tracings of some old foundations remaining show there was at one time a settlement. Even the road up that beautiful canyon, through which freight teams and other vehicles meandered in their day, is now next to impassable in places even to a burro. The place never achieved the dubious distinction of "ghost town," for when it started going down it seemed to go almost in a heap, like the Deacon's "one-hoss shay."

Mogollon, on the other hand, is valiantly hanging on, although its physical aspects have been altered by two fires in recent years. We still have the luxury of a post office and daily mail (except Sundays and holidays). There is still a lot of gold and silver ore in the mines

* This article was written by Mr. Hoover a year before he died on January 12, 1958.

hereabouts, but until present economic conditions change they could not be operated at a profit. Following the beginning of World War II, Federal requirements closed almost all gold mines in the United States. Operations ceased here on June 18, 1942. Since that time the wages for mine labor have quadrupled while the price of gold and silver has remained unchanged.

By the summer of 1950 someone was writing about Mogollon as a "ghost town" that was "for sale." The article appeared in a Silver City newspaper and seemed to take. Papers scattered over a wide area picked up the idea and reprinted the story's substance, though not always retaining its original spirit. One eastern paper went so far as to warn us that the Russians were buying up towns over here! However, to my knowledge no Soviet agent has yet appeared. There have been several sales in the past five years, seven or eight at least, including several El Paso buyers.

In October, 1950, I was in Scranton, Pennsylvania, where the home office of the Lehigh Metals Company (present owners of the Mogollon mining properties) is located. The president, John A. Hart, told me that he had been rather startled one evening to hear over his radio that "the ghost town of Mogollon, New Mexico, is for sale."

But Mogollon had made its mark as a ghost town. On September 9, 1950, a post card was addressed to me

> Mr. Hoover
> Bloated Goat Bar
> Ghost Town, New Mexico

Two days later I received the card.

That bar! One day someone, who was feeling his oats, with a piece of chalk sketched on the outer wall of the establishment a very good likeness of a goat swollen to distress. Someone else, seeing it, called the place "The Bloated Goat." The name stuck.

In its day the Bloated Goat was a rendezvous for old-timers, a place where many early-day events were re-lived with no little nostalgia. Such are the ways of men. But alas! like many another landmark in Mogollon, it is now only a memory. The wind and rain weathered away the chalk; it went out of business as a bar. Finally the building was sold, dismantled, and hauled away to Reserve, the county seat, for re-erection.

At the peak of mining activity more than thirty-five years ago, this area estimated its population at around 1800. Today within the two-mile radius of Mogollon that we call the community, there are only some twenty residents. Recently when I was in Silver City on my way home a friend asked me, "How many people are there in Mogollon?"

"Eleven now," I replied, "but this evening there will be twelve."

Even the wild life seems conscious of our sobriquet and its implication. Wild turkeys have been seen within a hundred yards of our residence here at the mine, only a mile from town, as well as at the edge of town itself. Once I saw a racoon in the yard here during the afternoon. Coming up the canyon road one evening in January, 1951, we surprised fifteen deer milling around a block of salt at the roadside about half way between here and Mogollon.

But the boldest of all was a visitor that came into the village on March 1st of that year. The postmaster, J. R. Wray, had about finished his work for the day when he heard his dog in a fight in front of the post office. On looking out he saw it was tangled up with a mountain lion. He kicked them apart, but the dog was so badly mangled that it had to be killed. The lion then went around behind the building. Fortunately, T. J. "Shorty" Lyon, my neighbor and a professional trapper and hunter for the United States Fish & Wild Life Service, arrived from his trap line a few minutes later with his constant companion, Button. The hound took the trail and about a half hour later Shorty shot the lion.

Lions are rarely known to come to human habitations. Cutting it open, Shorty found the stomach of this one empty, so it must have been extreme hunger that gave it courage to enter the village. We shuddered to think what might have happened had one of Mr. Wray's little boys been in the street at the time instead of the dog.

In the early twenties Socorro County was split up, this end of it becoming Catron County with Reserve as its county seat. The 1940 census gave our county a population of 4881; by 1950 it was reduced to 3533. Much of the decrease was the exodus from Mogollon in 1942 after the mines shut down.

With an area of 6898 square miles, larger than a couple of eastern states combined, Catron County has almost two square miles for every man, woman and child in it. Without a bank or a railroad, it is one of the few remaining frontiers of the West.

❊   ❊   ❊

And, finally—having lived the greater part of his life in such an environment that one might travel far to find another of like appeal—the author hopes to spend his remaining years in this Land of Enchantment, so appropriately named.

Mogollon scenery which Mr. Hoover loved

Mr. Hoover had several photographs similar to
the one above which he would show to visitors
and say, "this is a picture of my front yard." The
poem on the next page was one of his favorites.

GHOST TOWN

Where the mule deer bound through the forest,
    Wild turkey feed by the rills,
The scream of the hawk at twilight,
    The panther prowls in the hills—

Where the pines like giant arrows
    Point upward toward the sky,
And moon-bathed rocky pinnacles
    Resound the coyote's cry—

Where crumbling logs and timbers
    That once were happy homes
Is now the wild but lovely
    Ghost town of the Mogollons—

This is the place of contentment,
    A place in this Universe where
Confusion and fear are abandoned,
    For God is abiding there.

—DEL BARTON

EL PASO
TEXAS